YOU KNOW WHO

YOU KNOW WHO

BY JOHN CIARDI

Drawings by Edward Gorey

J. B. Lippincott Company

Philadelphia
New York

Printed in the United States of America

ISBN-0-397-31573-2

Library of Congress Catalog Card No. 64-19057

Sixth Printing

ACKNOWLEDGMENTS: "Calling All Cowboys" was originally published in *Ladies' Home Journal.*

This book is for

DESRA SONNEK

Myra's good friend and mine,
partly because of the way she
used to giggle, and partly because
she doesn't giggle quite that way
any more (she is growing up), and
mostly because watching her begin
to grow up has been a happy thing.

CONTENTS

POOR LITTLE FISH

There was a fish who was born in a cup.
He grew and he grew till he filled it up.

Then he sang all day, "Just look at *me!*
A bigger fish you will not see!"

Poor little fish!—he took his cup
To be a sea. When he filled it up

He shook with pride from head to tail.
He *really* thought he was a whale!

—Is there anyone here who acts that way?
I know someone, but I won't say.

CAN SOMEONE TELL ME WHY?

Someone under a chestnut tree
Got a bump on the head and he blamed me.

Now he is cross and so am I.
Is there anyone here who can tell me why?

11

SOMEONE ASKED ME

What do you think a kite would do
If someone cut its string in two
When it was flying high in the sky?
Would it go on flying? And if not, why?
If it did stop flying, would it drop?
How would it drop?
      Flip . . .
           Flip . . .
                Flip . . .
                     FLOP!

GET UP OR YOU'LL BE LATE FOR SCHOOL, SILLY!

Someone I know—and he's very near—
Someone I know who lives right here,
Someone I know with a pumpkin head,
Someone right here in *this* bed,

Would like me to think he is sound asleep.
Would like me to think he is far and deep
With his nose in the pillow. Would like me to think
I didn't see him—quick as a wink—

Duck back into bed as I came in.
I saw him all right. I saw him grin.
He is grinning right now. And how do I know?
Maybe a grin-bird told me so.

Or it just may be that his grin has spread
Around his face to the back of his head.
Why, so it has! Oh dear! Oh dear!
I've heard of grinning from ear to ear,

But never before have I ever found
A grin that goes the whole way round
The back of the neck. If he grins any more,
His head will fall off and roll on the floor.

Well, if anyone *is* there in that bed,
If anyone's home in that pumpkin head,
And if whoever it is, is you—
You had better get up!
        —Well! How do you do?

SOMEONE HAD A HELPING HAND

Someone I know had a helping hand.
He was helping himself to beat the band.

Yes, he was being a help to me:
He was picking the pears out of my tree.

I wanted to help him do it up brown.
So I took my saw and sawed it down.

He fell from the tree right onto his hat.
"Now why," he said, "did you do that?"

"That tree," I told him, "was very tall.
I was afraid, sir, you might fall.

"With your sack stuffed full of my pears—do you see?—
I wanted to help you down from the tree.

"For helping me was so kind of you
That it made me want to help you, too."

WHAT SOMEONE SAID WHEN HE WAS SPANKED
ON THE DAY BEFORE HIS BIRTHDAY

Some day
I may
Pack my bag and run away.
Some day
I may.
—But not today.

Some night
I might
Slip away in the moonlight.
I might.
Some night.
—But not tonight.

Some night.
Some day.
I might.
I may.
—But right now I think I'll stay.

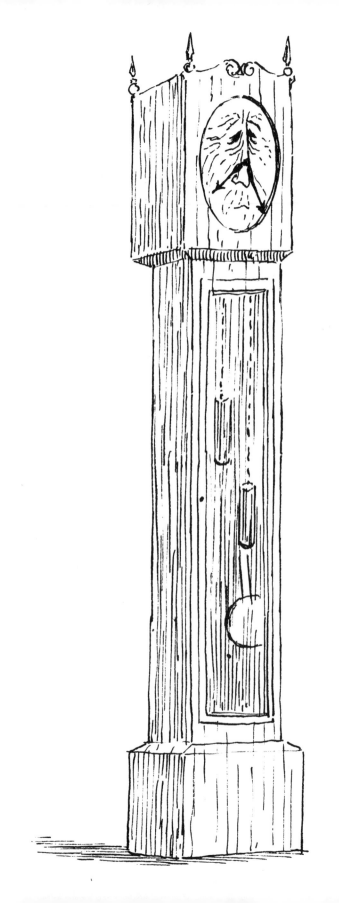

.20

SOMEONE SLOW

I know someone who is so slow
It takes him all day and all night to go
From Sunday to Monday, and all week long
To get back to Sunday. He never goes wrong.
And he never stops. But oh, my dear,
From birthday to birthday it takes him all year!
And that's much too slow, as I know you know.
One day I tried to tell him so.
But all he would say was "tick" and "tock."

—Poor old slow GRANDFATHER CLOCK.

SOMEONE MADE ME PROUD OF YOU

Someone—I forget just who—
Said there's *nothing* you can't do.
He said that you could tie your shoe,
See the sky when it is blue,
And count *all the way* to two!

My, but I was proud of you!
I hope that all he said was true!

AND OFF HE WENT JUST AS PROUD AS YOU PLEASE

Said Billy to Willy,
"You have a silly name!"
Said Willy to Billy,
"Our names are much the same."

Said Billy to Willy,
"That is not true.
Your name is silly,
Just like you.

"Your name's a silly shame.
My name is fine.
For my name, my name,
My name is *mine!*"

IT *IS* TIME, YOU KNOW

Someone I met
Downtown today
Wants me to say—
And I mustn't forget—

That someone here
Has mud on his nose,
And some on his toes,
And some in one ear.

Yes, someone right here.
Please scrub your toes.
Please scrub your nose.
Please scrub that ear.

—Did you do as I said?
Toes, nose, and ear?
Now can you hear?
Good—go to bed!

IF YOU SHOULD FALL, DON'T FORGET THIS

Someone big and someone small
Tripped and banged their heads on the wall.

Someone small got a little bump.
But someone big got a great big lump!

There is one good thing about being small—
You just don't have so far to fall.

And here's another—when you do,
You have less to pick up. Now isn't that true?

IS THIS SOMEONE YOU KNOW?

There was a boy who skinned his knees
Jumping over his father's trees.

He took a run and he took a jump,
And down he came with a skid and a bump.

The higher the trees the higher he jumped.
And when he came down the harder he bumped.

The harder he bumped the longer the skid.
But he jumped them all. He did, he did.

And every time he skinned his knees
He jumped again—as proud as you please.

Till he tried one day to jump over the sky.
But he

l
   a
     n
      d
        e
       d

           s
             o

hard it made him cry.

THE GREAT NEWS

Someone heard the whole town saying
    How good it was going to be.
Someone heard the band was playing
    "What a Great Day We Shall See!"

Down the street for blocks around
    Boys came running to find out.
When I told them what I'd found,
    My, you should have heard them shout!

Someone from the *News* came by
    To find out if it was true.
And away up in the sky
    Airplanes spelled it on the blue.

Someone called and said he heard
    It was going on TV!
And I heard a little bird
    Sing about it in a tree!

When the town heard it was true,
    All the bells began to chime!
They rang and rang the great news—YOU
    Went to bed when it was time!

SOMEONE WAS UP IN THAT TREE

Someone up in a tree—*that* tree—
Was shouting, "Hey! Just look at me!"

Why do I think he was being so loud?
Why do I think he was acting so proud?
Why was he shaking the tree for joy?
Oh, just to prove he was a boy.

There is nothing as loud as a boy in a tree.
There is nothing as proud as a boy in a tree.
It must have been a boy—*some* boy.

It *could* have been an ape—that's true.
It *looked* like an ape. But somehow I knew
It was just *part* ape—Was the other part you?

COME TO THINK OF IT

I know someone who lives at the zoo.
Someone who looks a lot like you.
. . . No, not the monkey nor the kangaroo!

. . . But come to think of it, the monkey *might* do.
That's not what I had in mind, it's true . . .
But, yes, come to think of it, the monkey *would* do!

BUMP! BANG! BUMP!

Someone—and I mean *you*, my sweet—
Runs around here on just two feet.
Just two, I know. But now and then
He makes two feet sound more like ten!

I don't see how two feet can use—
Not at one time—more than two shoes.
Yet let those two shoes in the door
To bump and bang across the floor
And two shoes sound like a lot more.
They sound, I'd say, like forty-four.

Two shoes on two feet—let me see:
How many small boys should that be?
Two feet—one boy. Right? But my word,
He sounds to me more like a herd!

—If he keeps going on this way,
I'll take him to the barn some day,
And lock him up and feed him hay!

CALLING ALL COWBOYS

Some of the cowboys I know best
Have never punched a cow out West.
Some don't have a cow to punch
(But they can eat most of a cow for lunch.)

Some of the fastest guns I see
Have never shot anyone on TV.
They have no stars, they have no chaps,
And all they have in their guns is caps.

Some of the bad-men I have met
Have never been out-laws. Well, not yet.
But I know one or two who *are*
Wanted—for robbing the cookie jar.

And of them all, there is one I like
Who keeps shooting the town up from his bike.
He's a cowboy, a bad-man, and fast on the draw.
And he's an out-late if not an out-law.

Don't get in his way. Or quick as a wink
He'll go for his gun, and he'll shoot you, I think.
But tell him I said there's a price on his head,
And I'm out to get him. He's wanted—for bed!

PLEASE!

Someone about
As big as a mouse
Runs in and out
Of *this* house
    TOO MUCH!

Someone about
As loud as a yell,
A bark, a shout,
A drum, and a bell—
    CLANG! CLANG!

Yes, it might be you.
It just *might* be.
And if that's true,
Take a tip from me—
    STOP IT!

SOMEONE AT MY HOUSE SAID

"Those things you have on the sides of your head—
One on this side, one on that—
Are ears," the man at my house said.
"What good are ears? Well, if your hat
Is a bit too big, your ears, you'll find
Can keep it from sliding down over your eyes
And making you think you have gone blind.
But if your hat is the right size,
Then the very best thing to do with ears
Is to hear what I have to say, my dears,"
(The man who lives at my house said)
"And what I am saying is—TIME FOR BED!"

A LOUD PROUD SOMEONE

Someone I knew was very proud.
But all he was proud of was—being LOUD.

When he said "Hello" it went BOOM-BOOM-BOOM
Like guns going off in a very small room.

He told me his name, but all I heard
Was BOOM-BOOM-BOOM—not another word.

"BOOM-BOOM-BOOM-BOOM-BOOM-BOOM," said he.
"Well," said I, "it seems to me
This BOOM-BOOM game can be played by two,
So a very fine BOOM-BOOM-BOOM to you!"

He shook my hand and he slapped my back
So hard I think I heard something crack.
And "BOOM-BOOM-BOOM," I heard him say.
And then—thank goodness—he went away,
With his hat tipped back and his head up, proud
Of nothing but being so BOOM-BOOM loud!

Well, let him be proud as he likes, I say.
Just so long as he stays away!

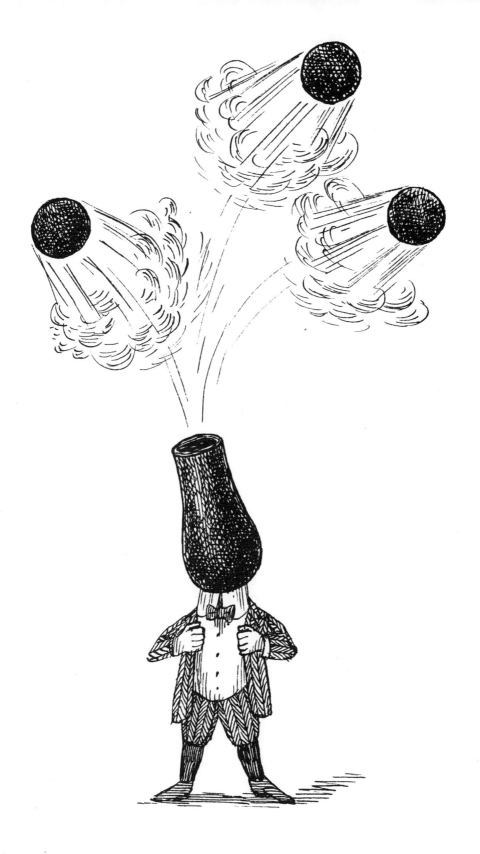

WHAT SOMEONE TOLD ME ABOUT BOBBY LINK

What do you think
Of Bobby Link?
He went for a swim with nothing to drink
But iced tea, hot tea,
Milk in a jug,
Cherry pop, coffee,
Beer in a mug,
And a hat full of rain,
And a cap full of snow.
He was never seen again.
And some who know
Say he got so wet
When he drank it all down
That he isn't dry yet.
—I hope he didn't drown.

PLEASE DON'T TELL HIM

I know and you know and Billy knows, too.
He knows what we know, and he knows that we do.

But does he know we know that he knows we know?
If he doesn't know *that*—please, don't tell him so.

SIT UP WHEN YOU SIT DOWN!

Someone about as big as a bump
Sat down to breakfast all a-slump
With his head in his hands and his chin in the plate.
"Sit up!" I said. "Yes, you. Sit *straight!*
Sit *up* I say!" I saw him frown.
"Sit up," I said, "when you sit down!"

He let out a *giggle.* He let out a roar.
He almost rolled around on the floor.
"How can I?" he said when he saw me frown,
"How can I sit *up* when I sit *down?*"

Well, what could I do? It was getting late.
And he hadn't eaten a thing from his plate.
I had to show him. I had to be quick
Or he'd miss school. So I got a stick . . .

And did I beat him? Goodness, no!
He took one look and he seemed to know
Just how to sit up when he sits down.
And now he's the very best boy in town!

SOMEONE SHOWED ME THE RIGHT WAY
TO RUN AWAY

Someone fast and someone slow
Ran away a year ago.

Someone fast—let's call him Jack—
Ran so far he ran right back.
He ran so fast that he ran away
And got back home all in one day.

Someone slow—let's call him Joe—
Ran and ran, but he was so slow
He still had all of his going to go.
He tried, he did—he ran on and on,
But he was so slow he never got gone.

He ran for hours, and maybe more.
But still he never got out the door.
He ran and he ran and when at last
He stopped—why, there came someone fast!
And that one—yes, his name was Jack—
Had run so far he had run right back!

So there they were—Slow-Joe, Fast-Jack—
Back in the house in time for a snack
And a game or two. And what I say
Is: if you *have* to run away,
Be like Jack or be like Joe.
Be someone fast or someone slow.

Run so slow that you never go.
Or run so fast that before you know
You're even gone, you find you're back
In time to have a little snack
And play a game—like Joe, like Jack.

SOMEONE LOST HIS HEAD AT BEDTIME
BUT HE GOT IT BACK

Someone said
That someone I knew
Had lost his head.
If it was you
He had in mind
(And if it's true),
I hope you find
A new head soon.
Most any kind—
An old balloon
Might have to do.
Or maybe the moon
(If you just knew
How to reach for it.)
Here's a pot of glue—
Just put a bit
On your neck bone—so.
Don't throw a fit—
It sticks, I know.
But here's a mop
That I think might grow
Good hair on top
If we stick it tight.
(I think it might.
That would be a sight.)

—OK, I'll stop.
You may be right.
Yes, that *could* be
Your head. At night
It's hard to see . . .
Put on the light.

Well, goodness me!
It's your head all right!
And back on tight!
That's a happy sight!
Well then, sleep tight.
Put out the light.
And so good night.

Kiss you? I might.
—There now. Good night.

One more? All right.
—There now. Good night.

One more?
GOOD NIGHT!

PLEASE TELL THIS SOMEONE TO TAKE CARE

Someone I know—
It might be you—
Has a hole in his shoe.
I can see his toe.
It goes peek-a-boo
In and out of his shoe.

Will you be so good
As to look at *your* shoe?
If it should be you—
Just *if* it should—
Will you tell me true
What you mean to do
About that shoe?

Whatever you do
It seems to me
You had best not go
Out into the snow
Or across the sea
With that hole in your shoe,
With that hole in your toe.
A snow-fox might
Just take a bite.
Or a wave or two
Might get into your shoe
And drown a toe.

Or that hole in your toe
Might grow and grow
Till your big toe
Fell right out through
That hole in your shoe.

Then a little toe
Might be next to go.
To go right through
That hole in your shoe.
And before you know
Just what to do,
The next to go
Might just be YOU!

Then what would we do?
If we looked in your shoe
And couldn't find you?
If *no* one we knew
Was in that shoe—
Not so much as a toe?
What would we do?
What could we do?
We could *think* about you
As someone we knew—
Or used to know—

We could wish that you
Had mended your shoe,
Had mended the toe.
What more could we do?
We might cry—that's so.
But what good would *that* do?

Don't let it come true.
Take care of your shoe
Before you fall through.

Or—goodbye! boo-hoo!

YOU KNOW WHO

You-know-who knows all there is.
And just to prove it, listen to this:

Some said to You-know-who,
"Three times what is twenty-two?"

You-know-who said, "Tut, tut, tut.
It's three times nothing at all, that's what!"

"But," said someone, "as I recall,
Three times nothing is nothing at all.

"And three times nothing-at-all won't do,
Unless nothing at all is twenty-two!"

"That's just what I mean," said You-know-who.

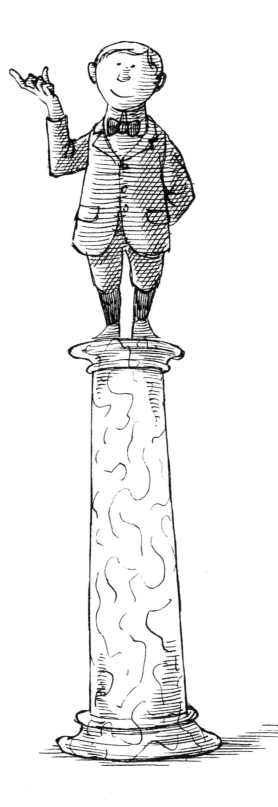